# The Thing-on-two-Legs

## Diana Hendry and Sue Heap

Collins

For Molly Green

## More Jets from Collins

The Thing-on-two-Legs
*by Diana Hendry and Sue Heap*

Georgie and the Computer Bugs
*by Julia Jarman and Damon Burnard*

Granny Grimm's Gruesome Glasses
*by Jenny Nimmo and David Wynn Millward*

Lost Property
*by Pat Thomson and Caroline Crossland*

First published by A & C Black (Publishers) Ltd 1995
Published by Collins 1996

10 9 8 7 6 5 4

Collins is an imprint of HarperCollins Publishers Ltd,
77/85 Fulham Palace Road, London W6 8JB

Text copyright © 1995 Diana Hendry
Illustrations copyright © 1995 Sue Heap
All rights reserved.

ISBN 0–00–675099–0

Printed in Great Britain by Clays Ltd, St Ives plc

# Chapter One

One morning Mulligan's Thing-in-a-Box did something surprising.

It stopped sitting in a box.

It began crawling about the house.

Since its arrival, a few
months ago, Mulligan
had enjoyed being the
proud owner of the
Thing-in-a-Box.

It had taken him some time to realise that the Thing-in-a-Box wasn't:

a) an alarm clock with arms and legs that went

WAH WAH

several times a day and night.

b) a hairless puppy.

WOOF WOOF

Mulligan now knew that the Thing-in-a-Box was a baby boy and his name was Seamus.

Seamus, Mulligan thought, was not unlike the spider plant that sat in a pot on the window sill and occasionally waved a few fronds about or grew a little fatter. Both were decorative but useless.

Of course Seamus was noisier than the spider plant.

Seamus burbled and gurgled and warbled and did his wah-wah-wah imitation of an alarm clock.

WAH WAH

And nor did he sit in a pot, like the spider plant.

Seamus sat in a box. In fact he had a lot of boxes. He had a box-on-wheels, a car box, a bed box, and a bath box on a stand.

TOP

When Seamus wasn't in one box or another, Mrs Millie Dembo (the love of Mulligan's heart and tummy) sometimes hung him up from a hook in the ceiling. Then Seamus bounced up and down and did a great deal of burbling and warbling.

Sometimes, Seamus came out of his box and sat or lay on the floor and waved his legs about. But that was all he did.

It was quite beyond Mulligan to understand why Mr and Mrs Dembo thought Seamus was so very, very wonderful.

They even praised him for eating
his dinner . . .

who's a clever fellow!

. . . whereas no-one ever praised
Mulligan for eating anything – least
of all the slippers, knickers and
teddies which Mulligan considered
to be very chewable items.

Nevertheless, Mulligan *was* proud of the Thing-in-a-Box. This was because when ever they all went out together with Seamus in his box-on-wheels, people stopped to admire them.

What a nice family!

What a lovely baby!

Mrs Dembo got all shy and smiley
when they said this. And Mr Dembo
straightened his
shoulders and
grew half an inch
taller. Mulligan
joined in. After
all, he was part
of this family
wasn't he?
The Thing-in-
a-Box was
as much his
as theirs.

So Mulligan waved
the plume of his tail as
grandly and airily as he could
as if to say, 'Oh yes, quite
the best baby ever!'
Though to himself he
added, 'as babies go'.

The loveliness of Seamus puzzled
Mulligan. Seamus had no soft, fine,
feathery fur. He didn't have a tail
to wag and wave. He had ears, but
they seemed of little use. He could
neither flap nor droop them or give
one a good scratching with his foot.
Seamus's ears just sat on either
side of his head doing nothing in
particular as far as Mulligan could
tell. As for his nose – well that was
so small it didn't seem worth
having. And he had no teeth at all!

When Mrs Dembo said to Mulligan,
'Who's a beautiful boy then?',
Mulligan thought that at heart,
Mrs Dembo loved him best and that
the Thing-in-a-Box was just an extra.

But quite a nice extra. One way and
another it was good
becoming a family
and having a
Thing-in-a-Box
of your own.

Or at least it was until the morning
Seumus stopped bouncing on his
hook and sitting in a box, and
began to crawl.

# Chapter Two

And once he'd started,
he couldn't stop.

At first Mulligan was very
impressed. Four legs, instead of
two, had always seemed much the
best way to travel to Mulligan.

It is true that knees and hands
aren't as good as four long legs
and four tough paws, but even
making allowances for this,
Seamus was so very
very slow.

It took him half a morning to crawl across the room. He couldn't leap or bound. He was always falling on his nose . . .

. . . or getting one leg trapped under his bottom . . .

. . . or getting stuck in a corner and not knowing how to reverse.

Then he just went WAH-WAH-WAH until someone came along, lifted him up and turned him the right way round.

It was all very disappointing to
Mulligan.

But not to Mrs Dembo.

Mrs Dembo clapped and cheered
when Seamus crawled all the way
into the kitchen and
sat down in front
of her and
grinned.

'You're the cleverest boy ever!'
said Mrs Dembo.

And when Seamus crawled up the
stairs, well, you'd think he'd
climbed Mount Everest the way
Mr and Mrs Dembo carried on.

'A journey to the top of the world!'
said Mr Dembo, sweeping Seamus
up into his arms and giving him
a kiss.

One day, when they were all out on a picnic, Seamus began to crawl about on the rug.

Now, perhaps we can get going thought Mulligan, and he raced across the field, hoping Seamus might follow.

But Seamus crawled a few metres off the rug then sat on his bottom and went WAH-WAH-WAH!

WAH WAH WAH

Mr Dembo laughed.
'He wants to follow
Mulligan,' he said.

Mrs Dembo picked up Seamus and cuddled him.

It won't be long before they can run about together.

But Mulligan had no such hopes. He lay down in the long, cool grass and thought, 'Why, oh why, didn't they get a puppy?'

And then something even worse happened.

Seamus gave up four legs and tried walking on two.

And as far as walks were concerned,
Proper Walks – up-and-down-hills-
along-country-lanes-and-through-
fields sort of walks, decent five-mile
sort of walks – well, they were over.
Over forever, Mulligan thought.

Being part of a family when you
can't do what you want
to do, didn't seem
quite so much
fun any more.

# Chapter Three

Mr and Mrs Dembo told everyone,

They made telephone calls to
distant grandmas and grandads.
They wrote letters to old school
friends.

If anyone had asked Mulligan, (which they didn't, of course), he would have said that what Seamus really did was

totter and tumble,
toddle and waddle,
lurch and stagger,
wobble and womble.

And they call that *walking*, thought
Mulligan, showing off his very best
Crufts trot, up and down the
garden path.

And the trouble was that now
Seamus was a Thing-on-two-Legs,
he didn't want to sit in a box any
more.

In particular, he didn't want to sit
in his box-on-wheels.

'Ow! OW!' he would cry (meaning
'Out! Out!') when Mrs Dembo
tried to put him in it.

OW! OW

So out he came to
totter and toddle,
wiggle and wobble,
VERY VERY
SLOWLY,
holding on to
Mrs Dembo's
hand while
she walked
VERY VERY
SLOWLY
too.

It could take an hour to get to the end of the road and by then Mulligan, who had also walked VERY VERY SLOWLY, was just about ready to burst with unspent energy. He wanted to run and race, spin and speed, pounce and bounce, scramble and ramble, rush and dash. Instead it was one paw two paws three paws four, V E R Y S L O W L Y like that.

As it was winter, the evenings were dark and Mr Dembo was too tired to take Mulligan out for a walk when he got home from work.

Most mornings Seamus had a nap and Mrs Dembo tidied up and got lunch ready. Mulligan went out into the front garden. By standing on his two back legs and leaning his front legs over the garden wall, he could watch the world go by.

In particular, Mulligan watched Mr Linden and Gary go by. Mr Linden didn't have a small Thing-on-two-Legs. Mr Linden just had Gary, his labrador.

And every day Mr Linden and Gary walked past on their way up the lane to the fields and the woods beyond.

And every day Mulligan watched
them. He watched them and
watched them with longing in every
feather of his fur and with every
beat of his heart. At last he could
bear it no longer.

He jumped over the wall and
followed them up the lane.

Two families, thought Mulligan,
might be better than one.

# Chapter Four

At first Mr Linden tried to
persuade Mulligan to go home.

'Off you go, old fellow,' said Mr
Linden. 'Your folks will be looking
for you.'

Mulligan sat on
his haunches
and drooped his
droopiest look.

45

Mr Linden and Gary walked on.

Mulligan knew
where they were
going. They were
heading for the woods –
the nice damp, leaf-soggy
woods that had the odd
rabbit to chase and the
most interesting smells
in all the world.

Mulligan sat and waited a while
and then on his softest, sneakiest
paws, stood up and followed.

He wasn't going to be
left out of *this* jaunt!
Not after all that
VERY SLOW
toddling.

Mr Linden
looked over his
shoulder. Mulligan slunk
down low in
the grass but
Mr Linden
spotted him,
laughed
and waited.

He looked at the name and address on Mulligan's collar. 'Well, Gary,' he said. 'I get the feeling that you and I have been adopted.' And then he said to Mulligan, 'OK, you can come with us. But I'm taking you home afterwards.'

Mulligan waved his tail with a
great swish as if to say, 'Yes, please.
That's just how I want it!'

Then they were
off, Mulligan
and Gary,
romping and
racing, rambling
and scrambling,
sniffing and
snuffing, running
in and out of
the trees, free as
the wind in the
wonderful woods.

50

Back at home, Mrs Dembo had finished preparing lunch. She lifted Seamus out of his cot, put Mulligan's *Chumpy Chumps* in his bowl and called him.

There was no answer. Probably
digging up an old bone she thought
and she called him again. Still no
answer.

With Seamus in her arms, Mrs
Dembo went out into the garden.
But Mulligan wasn't anywhere to
be seen.

WAH-WAH-WAH went Seamus.

And Wah-Wah-Wah went Mrs
Dembo – only not quite so loudly.

Where's my
beautiful boy?

wailed Mrs Dembo.

WAH
WAH
WAH

wailed Seamus,
as if that's just
what he wanted
to know too.

# Chapter Five

Mrs Dembo's beautiful boy was
having a wonderful romp in the
woods of course. But it wasn't long
before Mr Linden brought him home.

As they come up the lane,
Mr Linden could see Mrs Dembo
standing at the garden gate with
Seamus on her hip, calling
Mulligan!

'I'm awfully sorry,' said Mr Linden,
'but Mulligan sort of adopted us.
He followed us to the woods. My
Gary tends to be a bit slow and
ploddy but your Mulligan has
cheered him up no end!'

Mrs Dembo dried her eyes.
'Mulligan would cheer anyone up,'
she said. Seamus
beamed and
reached down to
tug Mulligan's tail.

'What a lovely baby,' said Mr
Linden. 'My wife died a few years
ago. I'm retired now and I feel
rather sorry that we never had any
children.'

Mrs Dembo dumped Seamus in Mr
Linden's arms so that she could
give Mulligan a welcome home hug.

Mr Linden looked very surprised
and very pleased. He felt
doubly adopted.

'Come and have some lunch,' said
Mrs Dembo. 'I've been worried
about Mulligan not getting enough
exercise. Seamus has only just
learnt to walk, you see. And he's
rather slow.'

Well, I'm happy to take Mulligan out with Gary and me, if I can come and see your Seamus now and again.

Ridiculous, thought Mulligan! It was quite amazing how ridiculous people could be! And he hurried to his bowl of *Chumpy Chumps*.

When he'd finished, he settled down for a snooze. Yes, they were ridiculous, people, but useful. And when they were your own people, well . . .

**Ridiculous!**

... Mulligan gave a deep sigh of contentment – well, you couldn't help loving them too.